For Sue, Nick and Wei. ~ Kim

√N®

aska

FREDDIE the FLY

BEE ON, -BUZZ OFF-

a story about
learning to focus
and stay on task

BUZZ BUZZ BUZZ BUZZ BUZZ BUZZ BUZZ BUZZ BUZZ

Written by **Kimberly Delude**

Illustrated by **Brian Martin**

Freddie the Fly: Bee ON, Buzz OFF

Text and Illustrations Copyright © 2019 by Father Flanagan's Boys' Home

ISBN: 978-1-944882-34-1

Published by the Boys Town Press
13603 Flanagan Blvd.
Boys Town, NE 68010

For a Boys Town Press catalog, call **1-800-282-6657**
or visit our website: **BoysTownPress.org**

Publisher's Cataloging-in-Publication Data

Names: Delude, Kimberly, author. | Martin, Brian (Brian Michael), 1978- illustrator.

Title: Freddie the fly: bee on, buzz off : a story about learning to focus and stay on task / written by Kimberly Delude ; illustrated by Brian Martin.

Description: Boys Town, NE : Boys Town Press, [2019] | Series: Freddie the fly. | Audience: grades K-5. | Summary: Freddie whirls around to and fro, buzzing from one distraction to another. His lack of concentration causes a real fright when he finds himself lost and alone at the zoo. Will that be the scare Freddie needs to finally take action and turn his BEE on and his BUZZ off?–Publisher.

Identifiers: ISBN: 978-1-944882-34-1

Subjects: LCSH: Flies–Juvenile fiction. | Attention in children–Juvenile fiction. | Distraction (Psychology)–Juvenile fiction. | Self-reliance in children–Juvenile fiction. | Self-management (Psychology) for children–Juvenile fiction. | Hyperactive children–Juvenile fiction. | Children –Life skills guides–Juvenile fiction. | CYAC: Flies–Fiction. | Attention–Fiction. | Self- reliance–Fiction. | Problem-solving–Fiction. | Time management–Fiction. | Conduct of life–Fiction. | BISAC: JUVENILE FICTION / Social Themes / Self-Esteem & Self-Reliance. | JUVENILE FICTION / Social Themes / Peer Pressure. | JUVENILE FICTION / Social Themes / Special Needs. | JUVENILE FICTION / Social Themes / Friendship. | JUVENILE NONFICTION / Social Themes / Self-Esteem & Self-Reliance. | SELF-HELP / Self-Management / General. | EDUCATION / Counseling / General.

Classification: LCC: PZ7.1.D458 F742 2019 | DDC: [E]–dc23

Printed in the United States
10 9 8 7 6 5 4 3 2 1

Boys Town Press is the publishing division of Boys Town, a national organization serving children and families.

My name is FREDDIE

and from the second I wake up, I am go, go, GO!

My body is always **tapping** and my wings are always **flapping**.

They go up and down so quickly that they make a **buzzing** noise.

BUUZZZZZZZZZZ

"**Bzzzzzz!**" they sing as I race for the door.

Suddenly, Mom shouts, "FRREDDDIE!"

I pause but my wings keep **flapping.**

"Yes?"

"Did you forget something?"

I try to think but my mind is blank.

She smiles and says, "Your shirt."

Oops! That was a close one! I zoom up to get it.

I'm just about to leave again when I hear, "FRRREDDDIE!"

"Are you forgetting something else?"

I have all my clothes and my backpack. What could it be?

Mom holds up a lunch bag.

Oh. Right.

You see, sometimes I move so quickly I forget things.

But it's not my fault. There are just too many distractions.

Like in art class yesterday.

There was this really cool trash volcano. I couldn't take my eyes off it, and as soon as Mr. Bugcasso stopped talking, I flew up to touch it... which **landed me in trouble.**

Because the entire time I was so busy staring at it, Mr. Bugcasso had been explaining that absolutely no one was allowed to touch it.

Or, during our spelling test. Mrs. Stinger had the ceiling fan on, and it was making such a cool sound! I started tapping along and making up my own rhymes. I got so caught up that I didn't hear any of the spelling words and had to stay in from recess to finish my test.

Today it's impossible to stay focused because we are going on a field trip to the zoo!

TAP
TAPPITY
TAP
TAPPITY
TAPPITY
TAP TAP TAP
TAP TAPPITY TAP
TAPPITY TAP
TAPPITY
TAP TAP
TAP TAP TAP
TAP
TAP
TAP
TAPPITY
TAP

On the bus, I feel my body begin to tap and my wings start to **flap...**

The **buzzing** is so loud now, and there are so many interesting things to see out the window, that I miss what Mrs. Stinger is saying.

With each **tap** and **flap**, a new thought races through my mind...

Tap: I should ask her what she said.

Flap: Are we there yet?

By the time the doors open, I've already forgotten what I was going to do.

I try to stand with the other kids but then I...

See a lion!
Oh look, tigers!
Are those bears?

I buzz from animal to animal, snapping pictures as I go.

Finally, a noise louder than the buzz catches my attention.

Grumble... *Rumble...*

It's my stomach and it's hungry!

I stop to ask someone
when we'll have lunch.

But everyone I know is gone.
I look left...
I look right...

I look up high and even way down low...

No one.

Getting **nervous,** I start to sweat.

A puddle forms at my feet.

"Excuse me. Do you need some help?" asks a Bumble Guide.

They are the bugs who work at the zoo.

For a second I forget what's wrong. And then it all comes crashing out:

"I–WENT–TO–LOOK–AT–THE–LIONS–
AND–TIGERS–AND–BEARS–
AND–NOW–I'M–HUNGRY–AND–
LOST–AND–I–DON'T–KNOW–
WHERE–MY–CLASS–IS!"

"Well," says the guide, "did your class have a special meeting spot?"

I think back to riding on the bus and realize that is what
Mrs. Stinger was talking about when I was looking out the window.

I hang my head.
"Yes, but I don't know where it is."

"Not to worry," the guide says.

"My name is Gus. We'll find them."

We go to Gus's office and my body **hums** back to life.

I somersault around the room.

"What's this trophy for?"

"Did you really go on a safari?"

"Is that a real...?"

"Whoa, hold up,"
Gus says. "One thing at a time!
We have to do what we came here for."

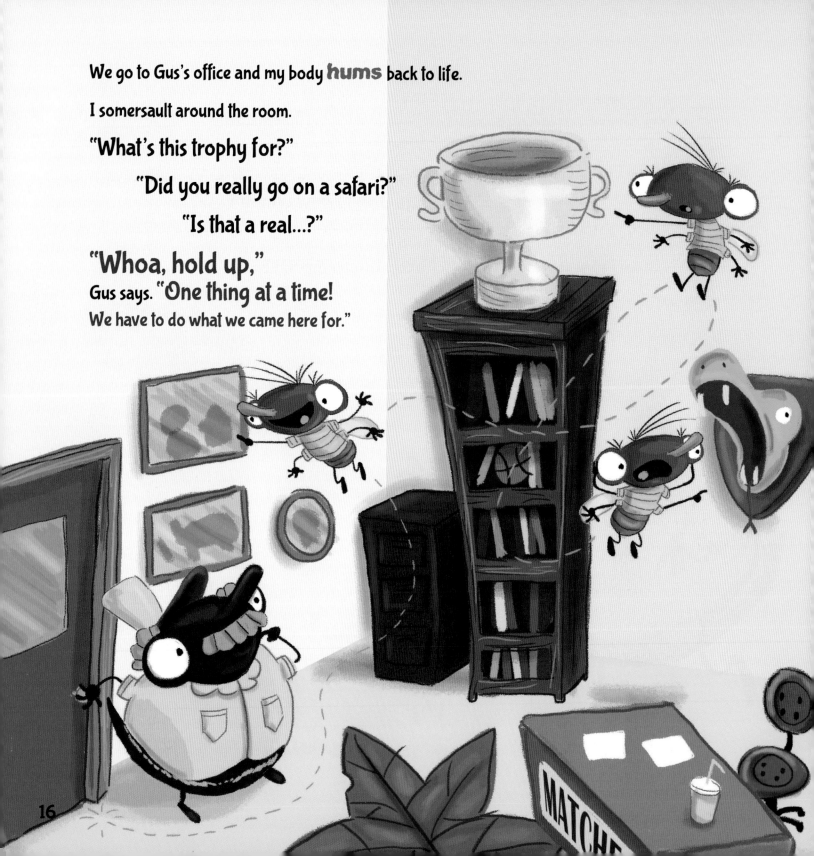

16

I stop.

What was that again?

Oh right! Finding my class.

"It seems like you have a hard time keeping your buzz under control and listening."

I nod as I eat one of his chocolate bug cookies.

"I used to be the same way."

"Really?"

"Really!"

"What did you do?" I ask.

"I learned to turn the **BEE ON** and turn the **BUZZ OFF**."

"Huh?"

MATCHES

Gus explained, "The **BUZZ** is your body. That constant *tapping~flapping* that keeps you moving makes it hard to listen.

But sitting still is hard for those of us who are

go-go-go.

What you need is to channel the buzz into smaller movements for those times you can't be moving.

Try this cater-wiggle band. You can **squeeze** and pull it while the rest of you stays in one place."

"**BEE ON** is your brain, ʜ ʜd ears.

These are what you need to ɪʜ

You have to look at the speaker, ʜen to what they say, and picture doing it in your mind."

"It seems really hard," I say.

"It will be hard at first," **says Gus.**
"Let's practice with a game of **BUZZ SAYS**."

19

"How do you play?" I ask.

"I'm going to give you an instruction. Before you do it, repeat it to yourself two times, and picture doing it in your head. Only after you do that can you do what I asked."

"Okay. Stand up."

As soon as the words are out of his mouth, I am up.

"Ooops! Sorry!"

ATCHES

20

"No apologies needed. It's going to take some time," Gus says.

Just then, Mrs. Stinger showed up and I started to hand Gus the band.

"Nope, you keep it as a reminder to **BEE ON** AND **BUZZ OFF**."

On the bus, Mrs. Stinger clears her throat.
"Everyone, when we get back, I want you to go to your spot on the rug."

I turn to look out the window but the band in my hand catches my eye.

I squeeze it and repeat Mrs. Stinger's instructions
two times while picturing myself doing it.

Bug to rug. Bug to rug.

By the time we get back to school, I can't remember what we are supposed to do.

Mesquita and I both stare at each other because she can't either. I can hear her body **buzzing** almost as loudly as mine.

Mrs. Stinger comes over and asks us if we remember the instruction.

I squeeze the band and remember the picture I took with my brain.

I say, *"Bug to rug!"*

Mrs. Stinger smiles. "That's a good strategy. It's also good to have a friend to help you stay on task. Try reminding each other if you forget."

Buzz

Buzz

Buzz

Buzz

Buzz

Buzz

Buzz

Then Mrs. Stinger starts talking to the whole class about our next assignment.

My body begins to **buzz** and my eyes wander around the room to see what everyone else is doing.

When I catch Mesquita's eye, she nods her head toward Mrs. Stinger, reminding me to listen. I squeeze the cater–wiggle band, turning my **BUZZ OFF** and turning my **BEE ON**.

"Class, I want you to do your trash sculpture first, and then you can splatter paint."

I repeat it twice and picture myself doing it: *Trash first, splatter second.*

It works! And for the rest of the day, Mesquita and I help each other to remember to **BEE ON** and turn our **BUZZ OFF**.

By the end of the day, I'm so tired that when I get home, I just fall on the couch.

From the kitchen Mom says, "Time to wash up and set the table."

I half listen as I stare at the TV screen.

Then I flit up the stairs, wash my hands, and race back to the couch.

The commercials have just ended when I hear Mom clear her throat.

Uh oh. I try to think back but I hadn't been listening.

I explain to her the **BEE ON, BUZZ OFF** skill I learned that day and told her I had forgotten to do it earlier.

"It's okay," she says. "That's why I make lists."

"You do?"

27

"Yes, everyone has trouble remembering things at times, so making a list of what you need to do is great because you can go back and look at it whenever you need a reminder.

See? Here's mine: ☑ GET GROCERIES
☑ MAKE DINNER
☑ SIGN FREDDIE'S REPORT CARD...

...Good thing we looked at this.
I almost forgot about your report card,"
she says.

When I get to school the next day, Gus, the Bumble Guide, is standing there smiling at me.

He has my camera!

"How's **BEE ON, BUZZ OFF** working?" he asks.

"It's hard," I say. "But I've got it. I'm pretty sure I won't forget things from now on!"

OFFICE

I head off to class.

"FRREDDDIE," Gus calls.

I pause and turn.

"Yes?"

"Did you forget something?" he says, smiling.

I stop and think.

And he points to the camera.

Oops!
Well, I'll ALMOST never forget now.

TIPS FOR PARENTS & EDUCATORS

All kids like to move, but some kids just can't seem to stop. These kids have a hard time sitting still at home and at school. They may seem inattentive. That's why it is important to teach them strategies for controlling their bodies and strategies for focusing.

Using the **BEE ON, BUZZ OFF** method that Freddie learned can provide kids with the tools they need to pay attention and remember important information.

Here are a few activities that can be used anywhere to help children focus their minds and bodies and be in the moment.

1. Talk with your child about her need to move. Does she need to move her whole body (around the classroom) or can smaller movements (like squeezing putty) help?

2. Explain why listening with your brain, eyes, and ears is so important. Emphasize how, in certain situations or jobs, not following the directions can lead to big problems. Think about and discuss what would happen if you skipped a step in a recipe or if there was an emergency and you didn't know the plan.

3. Make lists or drawings instead of just giving verbal instructions. For instance, have your child help you make a visual list for going to the grocery store, and refer to the list as needed.

4. Explain why eye contact and repetition are important. Just because someone is looking at you doesn't mean he is listening. Have your child repeat back the instruction or information before moving forward. If it is too much, break it down into smaller steps and keep checking in with him.

5. Play games like Simon Says or Memory that require your child to focus on details. Make the games more difficult by having Simon give multiple steps at once.

6. Make sure your child knows you are there to help, and that it's safe for her to communicate her needs to you as her parent or teacher.

FREDDIE's TIPS to turn the BEE ON and the BUZZ OFF

1. Channel the Buzz into smaller movements (squeezing putty, wiggle hand, etc.)

2. Listen with your brain, eyes, and ears. Picture yourself following the instruction.

3. Repeat the instruction quietly to yourself.

4. Rely on a friend to prompt you or help you remember.

5. Make a list.

For more parenting information, visit **boystown.org/parenting**.

BOYS TOWN®
Saving Children ⬩ Healing Families

Boys Town Press Featured Titles
Kid-friendly books to teach social skills

Downloadable Activities
Go to BoysTownPress.org to download.

978-1-9-44882-34-1

978-1-944882-25-9

978-1944882-17-4

978-1-944882-36-5

978-1-944882-29-7

A book series designed to help kids master challenging social situations comfortably and competently.

978-1-944882-14-3

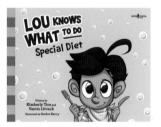

978-1-944882-15-4

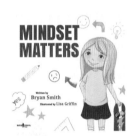

978-1-944882-12-9

978-1-944882-16-5

978-1-944882-26-6

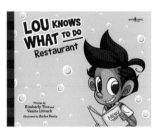

978-1-944882-27-3

978-1-944882-01-3

For information on Boys Town, its Education Model, Common Sense Parenting®, and training programs:
boystowntraining.org | boystown.org/parenting
training@BoysTown.org | 1-800-545-5771

For parenting and educational books and other resources:
BoysTownPress.org
btpress@BoysTown.org | 1-800-282-6657